Street Musicians on Postcards
A Picture Postcard Play

D1827274

A Picture Postcard Play compiled from a selection
of postcards depicting street musicians
of the late Victorian and the Edwardian eras.

Compiled and Edited by Paul Bellamy

978 - 0 - 9557869 - 1 - 4   MBSGB

Sponsored by the Musical Box Society of Great Britain, MBSGB
© 2008. ISBN978-0-9557869-1-4

Our thanks to past President Ted Brown for access to his collection of postcards

Preface

The picture postcard was, and still is, one of the biggest and most universal of collecting hobbies. It covers a whole range of social history from humour to the arts, from trade to transport, from stage to seaside entertainment. In doing so, the postcard helps to freeze in time a bygone age, now almost superseded by the internet, the email and the ipod.

The postcard evolved at a time when people used pen and ink to communicate via the postman's 'bike' and hand cart; when parcels and post-bags went by steam train, horse drawn wagon and the motor wagon; when ships carried goods to the far-flung corners of world and Empire. A time when three deliveries a day were the city norm; when the 'postie' was a welcome friend of town and village community; and when the Post Office was at the heart of that community.

This little book is dedicated to those times by concentrating on one aspect of the postcard era: the Street Musician. Like theatre, it has three acts, each with four scenes. During the two intermissions, read the programme notes while you eat your ice-cream or recline at the theatre's bar.

Introduction

This little book is about those street musicians who coloured our lives for over one hundred years. The monkey organ and the street barrel piano were common sights in the 1800s and the early 1900s. When people had time and money to go to the seaside or have a day out, the picture postcard became a popular way to tell family and friends. Street artists and musicians entertained us; the busker, the organ grinder and the hurdy-gurdy man had long since featured in western culture and it is no wonder that they found their way onto the picture postcard. For those who 'earned their corn' as street musicians but could not play a note, mechanical organs and pianos were the instruments of choice. In fact, with the advent of the pianola and the player organ, mechanical music featured indoors as well.

Many of these instruments survive to this day and new ones are still being made for our entertainment. We play them at organ rallies and street festivals all over the world but the reality of those times was very different. The life of the street musician was harsh. They pushed and carried their treasured instrument in all weathers, just to scrape a living. The story of Christie's Old Organ, by Mrs. O. F. Walton, epitomised the hardships they endured. The fact that the instruments survived in all weathers is also a testament to the craftsmen who made them.

The range of subjects and much that was written on post cards form part of our social history. Cards were often kept for years and the habit of collecting them became a hobby in its own right. Photography, printing technology and mass-production also played its part in post card production. Thus we start our picture tour of musical entertainment with Act 1, Scene 1: Hampstead Heath, or 'Amsted 'Eaf, as a Cockney lad would call that great open space on London's doorstep.

About the Musical Box Society of Great Britain

Musical Box Society of Great Britian (MBSGB) was founded in 1962. It has an international membership and close links with similar societies all over the world. We call ourselves the Musical Box Society because that is what we are, a container of music! Music of all types, music produced by means of a pinned barrel, a punched paper roll, a punched cardboard book and even the midi system so long as it operates a musical instrument. Thus, there are fairground organs, street pianos and organs; motorised, pedal-operated and hand-cranked pianos and organs, once so popular in the 19th and early 20th centuries; and we must not forget the musical box itself.

There is something for everyone in our society of collectors, restorers, computer wiz kids, model makers and hobbyists and those who just want to experience every conceivable type of music from jazz to operetta, from music hall song to concert repertoire. We have weekend meetings, overseas tours, house meetings and our quarterly journal,

The Music Box.

Go to www.mbsgb.org to find out more.
Single membership is not expensive and includes four superb journals each year. Joint membership is only a few pounds more. Membership Secretary: MBSGB PO Box 373, Welwyn AL6 0WY, UK. Tel: (Overseas code less the zero) 01536 726759
Email: kevin_mcelhone@hotmail.com.

Street Musicians on Postcards   A Picture Postcard Play

Index

Act I   Scene I
Hampstead Heath

Hampstead Heath is a well known landmark close to the centre of London in the borough of Camden. It is the same borough that housed Nicole Frères, one of the greatest names in Swiss musical box production, when it was moved from Geneva to Ely Place in 1880.* The heath is a vast stretch of open land, yet within sight of the centre, as can be seen from the highest part called Parliament Hill. The land was excavated in the 17th and 18th centuries with 30 reservoirs to supply London, six of them very large. Fairs are still common place now as then. These photographs reflect the pastimes of more sedate days.

The Nicole Factor in Mechanical Music
ISBN 0-9505657-3-3, published by MBSGB

ORGAN AND DANCERS. HAMPSTEAD HEATH.

"THE COSTER'S DELIGHT"

Copyright.

Postcard 1

Ladies with long skirts and large floral hats; men with winged collars, cloth caps, neckties and 'chokers', striped waistcoats; all so different from today's dress code of shabby Jeans. This was Hampstead Heath of yesteryear, when the costermongers had a day of celebration and relaxation. The Costers were London's barrow boys, selling fruit, vegetables, jellied eels and shell fish, particularly cockles and whelks; all part of London's traditional Cockney fare. The photograph is entitled 'Organ and Dancers, the Coster's delight', published by G. D. & D, London, the Star series, circa 1901.

314 Bank Holiday on Hampstead Heath.

Postcard 2

Printed by H. G. & L in their Living London series, another typical view of ordinary Londoners enjoying a brief holiday on the Heath. Circa 1900, the card is entitled 'Bank Holiday on Hampstead Heath', No.314. The writer shows that postcards were bought solely as a gift to others: Thank you for the nice PC you gave me. I hope you like this one. With love from Winnie.

DANCING ON SPANIARD'S ROAD, HAMPSTEAD HEATH.

Postcard 3

Another view of the Heath by an unknown maker but denoted as The Auto-Photo series and posted in 1909. Notice that the picture has been cropped from a larger photograph and put onto a plain background simulating the sky. Also, although the dancers are moving, their image is quite clear but the two lads on the left must have been too quick for the timed exposure. The picture is entitled 'Dancing on Spaniard's Road, Hampstead Heath'.

Act I Scene 2
English Street Scenes

The street musician may have been a welcome sight to many but an irritant to some. The barrel piano, often mistakenly called a barrel organ or hurdy-gurdy, was an exception. Both organ and piano had a limited repertoire but the piano often went out of tune; so much so that many towns and cities enacted bye-laws to ban them and punish the poor souls trying to scrape a living. When the instruments were 'in fine fettle' the sound of the music could be entrancing. Little monkeys were a common adjunct to attract both young and old, hence the term 'monkey organ'. The box seen straddling the hand-cart shafts of larger instruments often housed these little creatures. Contrary to popular opinion, these pets were often treasured and cared for by their owners, if only for the fact that their survival earned them a living and they were company to their owner's often-lonely lives.

Postcard 1

Entitled 'Dancing to organ', this scene probably depicts a barrel piano. The 'organ grinder' stands well in front of the instrument and seems to be turning a small handle, typical of the street barrel piano. The black & white photograph lacks a certain amount of realism and is probably partly staged. Also there are signs that the image has been touched up in places by hand, particularly some of the faces and the background. The location is not known but the card is by G. D. & D, London, called The Star Series. Early 1900s.

ROCKINGHAM ROAD, KETTERING

Postcard 2

This delightful black & white photograph is a view of Rockingham Road, Kettering. The poor chap grinding the barrel piano does not have much of an audience, most getting on with their business. The streets are empty of vehicles except for two hand carts. A man climbs a ladder; another carries bill boards and strolls past without a glance. Printed in England by C. F. P-N and posted in December, 1917. Of course, this was towards the end of The Great War, when most of the men and even teen-age boys were fighting and sacrificing their lives in that dreadful war.

Postcard 3

This black & white photograph is circa 1900 but reproduced as a postcard in 1977 by Tandem Publishing, No. P0045, printed in Wales. It is entitled 'The Hurdy Gurdy' which, of course, it is not.

Postcard 4

This black & white photograph is extremely good with high definition and depth of field. It is a view of the High Street, Market Harborough. The card is by P. L. N. Ltd, No. 813, printed in Saxony. Although there are no cars to be seen, note the garage sign just behind the organ grinder. Early 1900s and thought to be somewhere in the North of England because the words Manchester and Bradford appear on an advertisement painted on the side of the building on the right.

Street Musicians on Postcards

A Picture Postcard Play

Postcard 5

These two photographs have the same image, the top in black & white and the bottom in colour. Both are by P. M. & Co., London. The black & white version was printed by Armanio Bros., Genoa and the coloured version was printed in Germany. Entitled The Street Organ, it is almost certain that it is, in fact, a barrel piano. The images are quite crisp and are probably a London scene. It is certainly an English image because the 'organ' grinder has a placard around his neck with the word 'blind'. He also has a stick in his right hand but quite how this gentleman manages to push the heavy cart on cobbled streets is a mystery. The details are particularly interesting with the 'penny farthing' perambulator so high off the ground that it looks quite dangerous to the infant inside. Then there is the boy with the large tin bath on his back, the two ladies with their jugs and the little boys with ruffed collars; and all the women wear hats! The postal dates are 1902 and 1903, postage being ½ pence for 'inland' and 1 penny for foreign. One card is written 'Still getting on all right with good weather – quite warm today – London quite full'. Another was posted in Highbury, written in French and posted to Paris.

Street Musicians on Postcards

A Picture Postcard Play

Postcard 6

This fine coloured postcard is a good example of the street organ grinder. The bearded gentleman with weather-beaten kindly-looking face and floppy broad-brimmed hat is typical of the Italian itinerant street musician. The photo is entitled 'London Life. An Italian Organ Grinder'. The card is by Raphael Tuck & Sons, Oilette series No. 9015. Post dates of 1905 and 1906 are known. These 'oilettes', a trade name of Tuck, were copies of paintings.

Street Musicians on Postcards

A Picture Postcard Play

Postcard 7

A charming Edwardian scene, about 1902. A man plays a penny whistle behind the street organ. Illustrated by Sauber, from a series 'Familiar figures of London, No. 8, The Street Organ'. Printed in England but posted in Wien (Vienna) to Uncle Gunster of Vienna and written in German. Note the writer has marked a cross alongside the three golden balls, the sign pawn-broker's sign.

Act I   Scene 3
Ford and Barris - from Street to Stage

These four black & white postcards depict photographs of two smart young street performers and their barrel piano. The maker of the postcards is unknown so one wonders if the two lads were engaging in a bit of self publicity. Note that, in fig. 4, the two become three! Known as Ford and Barris but also as Ford and Barras, no doubt due to a printer's error. These two young men made it from street to stage, the Music Hall being the typically British form of entertainment of these early days. When Cinema caused the demise of the music hall, the 'end-of-pier' summer entertainment partly took its place

Postcard 1

This describes the pair as in the title of this scene, adding 'These boys a few weeks ago were working in the streets of London and are now creating a sensation in all the principal music halls'. Obviously they had a good agent to have performed in so many music halls in just a few weeks – but then that's show business.

Postcard 2

The same caption but a photograph in front of a different Inn. Maybe turning- out time was their main source of income!

Street Musicians on Postcards

A Picture Postcard Play

FROM STREET TO STAGE!

FORD AND BARRIS

Found performing in the streets of London, and immediately booked for all the principal Variety Theatres.

Postcard 3

With a change of name they now become Ford and Barris, the real and correct spelling for the duo. Now the legend reads 'Found in the streets of London and immediately booked for all the principle Variety Theatres'. Not only a change of name but a change of venue, except that a Variety Theatre was much the same as a Music Hall but sounds slightly more pretentious.

FORD & BARRIS TRIO.
Found performing in the streets of London now creating a sensation in all the Principal Music Halls.

Postcard 4

The duo becomes a trio. Note the background which advertises 'Good stabling'! For horses, one presumes but the actor's boarding house with its fearsome landlady was hardly better by reputation!

Act I   Scene 4
Comedy Photographs and Adelina Patti

The comedy photograph was invariably staged and the stage was often a photograph of a street scene. These examples may make you wonder how it was done. Perhaps a mask or a touch-up in the studio?

Street Musicians on Postcards

Postcard 1

'Steady on, Marie! Come down a notch, not so much like Patti*, more like Eva Tang!!!' The humour is lost today. Patti was a noted soprano and Eva had a deep voice, two performers of old, long since forgotten to most of us. This photograph was taken and published in 1910 by Bamforth & Co, England and New York, series No. 1644, printed in England.

A Picture Postcard Play

"Don't give the penny to the monkey, mother; give it to his father."

Postcard 2

'Don't give it to the monkey, mother; give it to his father.' Although the features of the organ grinder have been 'doctored', the photograph is real but the monkey is not! Note the tramlines and, behind, the Dispensing Chemist shop. Again, this postcard is by the same maker as in fig. 1, posted in 1912.

Street Musicians on Postcards

PARODIES OF THE LATEST PANTOMIME SONGS.
"Oh! Oh! Antonio."
Chorus by a victim:

"Oh! Oh! Antonio,
That tune all day
Oft makes me moan-i-o,
Even when alone-i-o;
Where'er I go the tune is sure to start;
I'm sick of 'Oh! Antonio' and his ice-cream cart."

Postcard 3

A Valentine series entitled 'Famous Throughout the World', featuring music hall songs, this one a parody of 'Oh! Oh! Antonio'. Italians were noted for their contribution to the British way of life not only as street musicians but also for the ice-cream cart. The background to this photograph is a stage set but the barrel piano, almost out of sight, is real enough although rarely used to accompany song (unless by Ford & Barris!)

Postcard 4

Probably Czechoslovakian and posted in 1908, this appears to be another stage-set photograph of children at play and doing things more basic to life!

*Adela (Adelina) Juana Maria Patti (1843 – 1919) was born of a Sicilian father and an Italian mother in poverty in Madrid. The family loved opera and moved to New York in 1847, living amongst the Italian community who recognised and supported her huge talent. Patti soon became a famous opera star, perhaps the first of today's superstars. She sang for President Abraham and his wife Mary Lincoln. Mary had lost a child to typhoid. The song that Adelina sang was Home Sweet Home, from Sir Henry Rowley Bishop's opera Clari, The Maid of Milan. Bishop wrote the music in 1823 and American John Howard Payne wrote the words. Lincoln, and no doubt Mary, was moved to tears and asked for an encore. She was truly a Maid of Milan and the song became her hallmark. At the age of 18, in 1861, she went to England and sang in the opera Sonnambula, by Bellini, at Covent Garden. La Sonnambula, the sleep-walker, was a favourite.

She travelled and sang all over the world. She also sang many Italian operas by Bellini, Donizetti, Rossini and Verdi; all popular composers to be found, metaphorically speaking, on many musical boxes.

Patti married a Marquis, not the tent of that name but one of the 'Landed Gentry'. She settled in South Wales at her estate called Craig-y-Nos, not with her husband but with her agent! Her first recordings, at the age of 63, were on the cylinders and discs of 'the talking machine' (the phonograph and gramophone). Despite the poor technical quality of this medium, she no doubt helped to put the musical box into history because these first recordings are said to reflect the superb quality of her voice, even at the age of 63 and more.

Adelina Patti carried on singing almost to the end of her life and died at her beloved Craig-y-Nor.

First Intermission

The Hurdy-Gurdy. Never the name for a barrel organ or barrel piano! It is a violin with rotating discs instead of a bow but still requiring digital dexterity to produce a tune.

The Postcard. An American invention. Here, or there, depending upon the reader's country of birth, it is called deltiology and ranks amongst the largest of the world-wide collecting hobbies, beaten only by philately (stamp collecting to you) and coin collecting (OK, numismatology, if you insist).

First Intermission
The history of the postcard

The precursor to the postcard was the picture-printed envelope, first produced by a D. William Mulready, Richard 'Dicky' Doyle, a Mr. E. R. W. Hume and the famous James Valentine. This was about 1840 to 1870. However, J.P. Carlton took out a US copyright in 1861 for a printed card and then transferred the rights to H. L. Lipman. By 1873, the US government intervened and displaced this private copyright with the U.S. Government Postals.

The UK 'penny post' was soon to be exploited because the picture postcard became a popular and cheap way to communicate. Introduced in England by Sir Rowland Hill in 1840, the Penny Black, with its image of Queen Victoria's head, changed the nature of the postal system. Before this time, the recipient had to pay but now the government benefited by this pre-payment system.

In 1869, Austria was the first country to accept the first "non-Postal" postcard, meaning a privately made postcard where postage had to be affixed. The Hungarian government accepted the postal card concept, suggested the previous year by Dr. Emanuel Herrmann, in 1870. The UK followed in 1872 and Germany in1874. By 1873, the US produced the first pre-stamped post cards. Advertising postcards first appeared in England in 1873. The first multicoloured card appeared in 1889.

The term 'postal card' defines a pre-paid state production and 'post card' defines a private production needing a stamp to be affixed. However, the word 'postcard' is well understood to be the pre-printed private variety. The US government charged the standard 2 cent letter rate for privately printed cards, the state ones being 1 cent. By 1898, more US regulation allowed the publishers to endorse their cards 'Private Mailing Card' at 1 cent but, as with government postals, writing was permitted on the picture side only. By 1901, the US required 'Post Card' to be printed on the address side of the card in lieu of the words 'private mailing card'.

Other countries had different ideas. October 1894 was thought to be the date when British postal authorities accepted British postcards as legitimate postal items in their own right. By 1899, the UK standard size for the postcard was 5½ x 3½ inches. In 1902, the UK permitted writing on the address side of the card by dividing it in two, the left side for writing and the right for the address.

France followed in 1904, Germany in 1905 but the US did not budge until 1907. Strangely, most US postcards were printed in Europe and many examples are found in this book, using a multiplicity of foreign languages, all saying 'post card', on each card! Germany was particularly noted for the quality of art work and the US responded with the oft- used protectionist policy of 'The Import Tariff', a technique also used for the mechanical musical instruments as well as general imports of other nature, thus spawning their home-grown products.

If a postcard has not been through the postal system or has had its stamp removed by an avid stamp collector, identifying the date of manufacture can be a problem. Many were reprinted long after the first issue date. With a postal stamp, things are a little easier but it is surprising that UK postal charges remained constant for up to forty years. They are as follows:
1st October 1870 to 3rd June 1918, ½ a penny (1d)
3rd June 1918 to 13th June 1921, one penny (1d)
13th June 1921 to24th May 1922, 1½d.
24th May 1922 to 1st May 1940, 1d.

One can imagine that the costs were affected by the close of the First World War and again by the beginning of WWII.

The photographic postcard started in 1900 and by 1906 Eastman Kodak produced a 'Folding Pocket Camera'. It enabled standard postcard-size black & white photographs to be copied directly onto a postcard. Other firms soon followed. One could even use a metal stylus to inscribe the negative with handwriting. This was the beginning of the personalised postcard.

By 1907, Europe exported 75% of its postcard production to the US. By now, the popularity of the postcard had escalated. World-wide, it was the biggest collecting hobby of all time. Nearly 678 million postcards were mailed in 1908. Technology then intervened once more. Just as the cylinder musical box and then the disc musical box declined with advent of gramophone, radio, so the postcard craze started to declined with the advent of the telephone. By World War I, the supremacy of German postcard production was lost for ever.

A Picture Postcard Play

SAY! LIFE'S NUTHIN' BUT
A DAMN GRIND, AIN'T IT?

Printed in the USA.
Two different 'grinders'. The knife grinder was a common sight, often with a bicycle that, when on its stand, drove the grind-stone by pedalling. This postcard looks typically British but is actually printed in the USA, where postcards began. Drawn by E. W Gustin, 1910. Printer unknown, series No. 5001.

Act II, Scene 1
The Staged Photographic Postcard

Unlike the staged photographs in the last scene, using the street and kiddies playing on a stage, those shown below were designed more as a series and usually for an anniversary. They often feature children and song.

THE MISTLETOE BOUGH.

The mist-le-toe hung in the cas-tle hall. The hol-ly branch shone on the old oak wall: And the

Bar-on's re-tain-ers were blithe and gay, And keep-ing their Christ-mas ho-ly day.

Postcard 1

The mist-le-toe hung in the cas-tle hall,
The hol-ly branch shone on the old oak wall;
And the Bar-on's re-tain-ers were blithe and gay.
And keep-ing their Christ-mas holy day.

These charming words are rarely sung today. The little boy in knickerbocker-type 'breeches', that seem to have been cut-down from adult trousers, cranks the organ whilst both the little girl and their monkey friend look a little bored! This colour-tinted photograph is circa 1904. It is unglazed and typical of this type. It is one of a series, printed in Germany but the maker is unknown. The obverse reads: Christmas Greeting: old tunes are sweetest, Old friends are surest. With every good wish for a happy Christmas.

Postcard 1

Postcard 2 & 3

These glazed, un-tinted, black and white photographs have the same little boy in two different poses, alone with the monkey who sits atop the organ eating the crumbs that were on his plate, which now serves as a collection plate.

I sat 'midst a migh-ty throng,
With-in a pal-ace grand,
It's a ci-ty far be-yond the sea,
In a dis-tant for-eign land,
I lis-ten'd, the grandest strain,
My ear had ever heard,
En-rap-tured, charm'd, amaz'd I was.
My in-most soul was stirr'd.

Street Musicians on Postcards

Postcard 2

A Picture Postcard Play

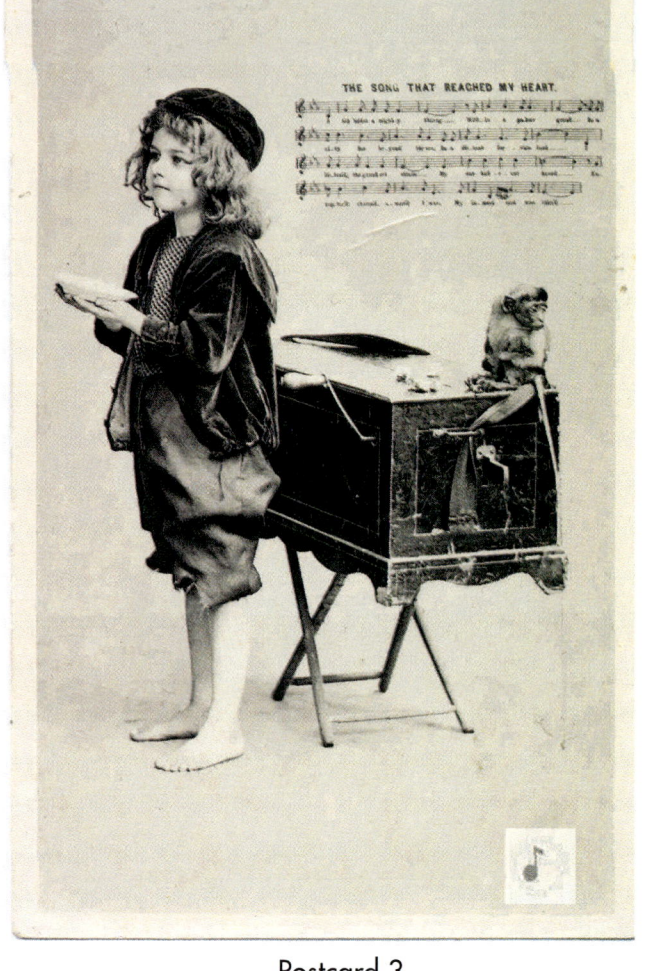

Postcard 3

A Picture Postcard Play

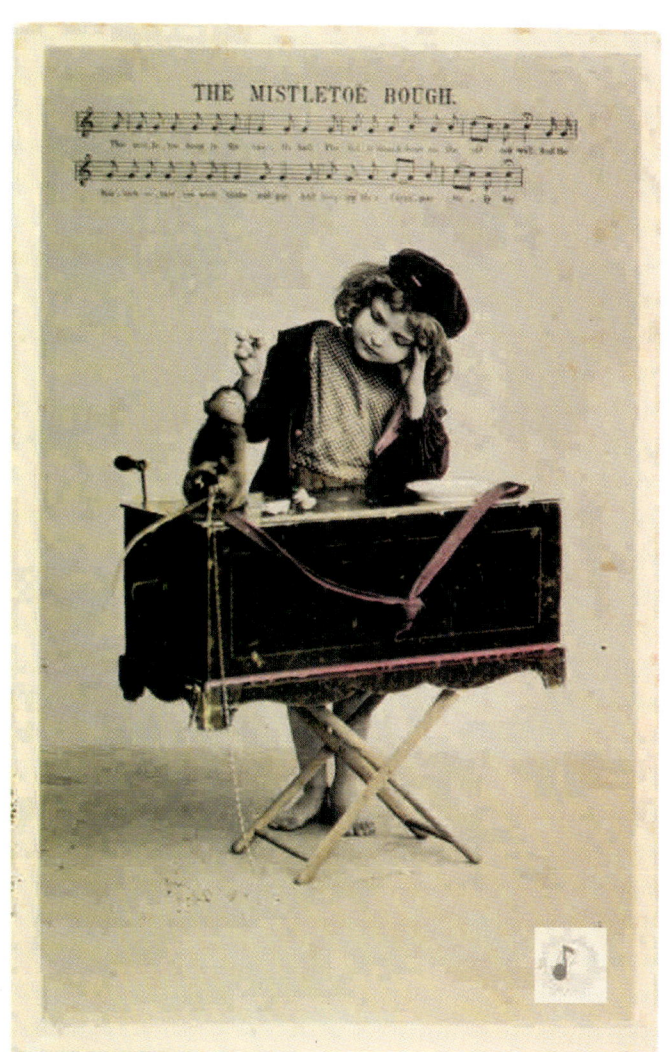

THE MISTLETOE BOUGH.

Postcard 4

Another unglazed and tinted version of our little friend and his monkey. This one was franked about 1906 at 12.1am, December 25, in Scarborough. It seems that the postal service was still active on this holy day. Aptly, the address is Miss Messenger, 41 Sandside, Scarborough.

Even in England, one needed only the briefest of address for the local postman, usually a 'pillar' and friend of the local community to ensure that the post arrived promptly, a far cry from our high-tech modern day with its first-class cost and second class service with barely once-a-day delivery. Of course, the postman, milkman, baker's boy and all those other important folk who truly supplied a service, would be rewarded with their Christmas box, just a few 'coppers' perhaps, by their grateful customers.

Street Musicians on Postcards

A Picture Postcard Play

Postcard 5

The last one in this series to be illustrated is the same boy in a similar pose. Another tinted card, it was not posted but used as a Christmas card and simply signed: From Grannie (to) Jamie, Xmas 1906.

The obverse of all the above in this series carried different versions of a Christmas Greeting: Christmas Wishes - may this Christmas in its flight leave you only pleasures bright; A happy Christmas - may harmony and peace be with you throughout the days of Christmas; A Christmas Wish - that Christmas time be glad and gay, and health and pleasure with you stay; Hearty Greeting - A merry Christmas, Good health and peace, And may your Happiness, Ever increase.

Postcard 6A

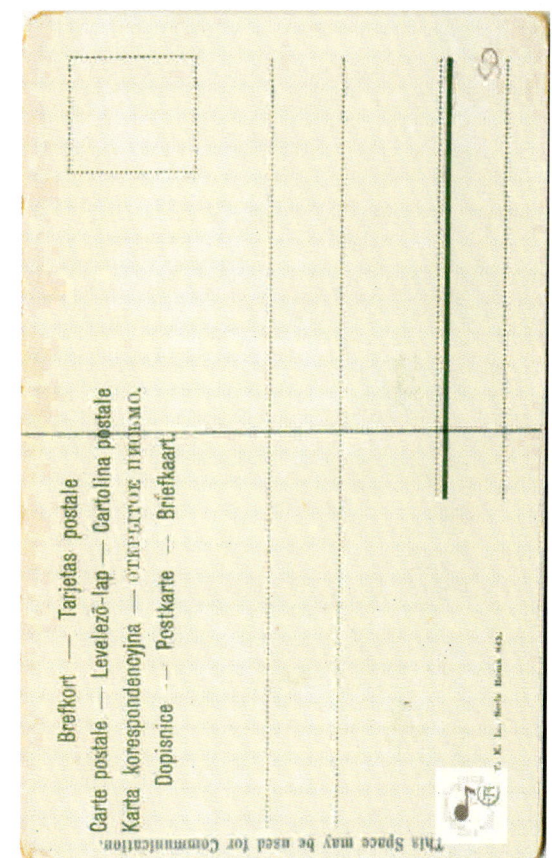

Postcard 6B

This photograph, fig. 6A, is extensively colour-tinted with a scenic background and, with the exception that proves the rule, is glazed. The obverse, fig. 6B, shows that it is intended for use in many different countries because of the different postal authorities listed. This was quite common at the time. The maker is 'T. E L., Serie Roma 845', (see fig. 7A).

Street Musicians on Postcards

A Picture Postcard Play

Postcard 7A

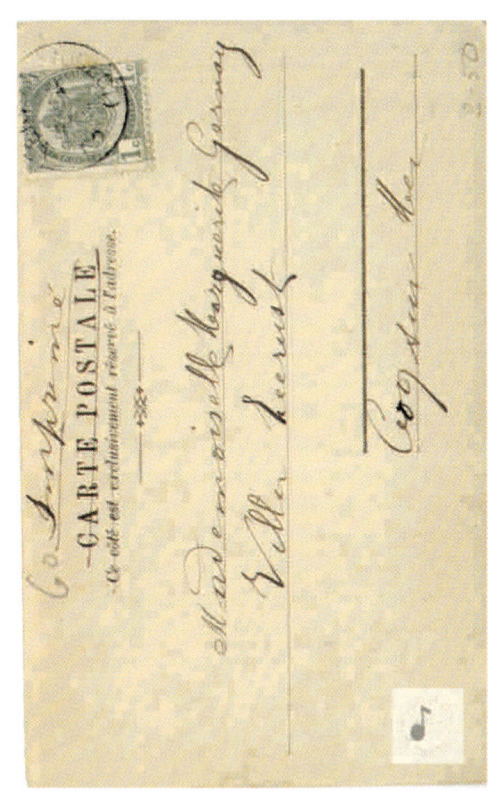

Postcard 7B

This black and white unglazed postcard has the same image as fig.6A but no background. The front has the legend: Serie 704, Clement, Tornier & Cie, Geneve. Thus we now know who printed 6A! Fig. 7B has a different format to that of 6B with no provision whatsoever for a message because it declares: Ce coté est exclusivement reserve à l'addresse (This side is exclusively reserved for the address) It was posted in Belgium in 1902.

It seems that the Geneva maker of Figs. 6 & 7 produced both cheap and more expensive versions for countries with different postal regulations.

Postcard 8

This is a delightful and rather unusual posed, colour-tinted but unglazed photographic postcard. It even has 'pearl buttons' all over her skirt, comprising hard white paint spots, each having a tiny black spot to represent the button's thread. Note also the five sealing-wax seals on the envelope held in the dog's mouth.

The only indication of the maker is a small cartouche on the obverse containing the letters P. R. A. within a circular swag of flowers, all printed in red. The obverse is written in French from Sam to his brother, circa 1905/6.

Street Musicians on Postcards

A Picture Postcard Play

Postcard 9

Another version of a Christmas postcard and 'A Song That reached My Heart'. This unglazed colour-tinted photograph is of another little boy in knickerbockers, this time with a toy monkey on his back. The obverse states that it was printed in Germany but the maker is unknown. Unstamped and thought to be circa 1900/05, it was obviously given as a Christmas card by 'Auntie Lyd to Master Reggie'.

Postcard 10

Is this a Photograph? The illustration is from Galerie Rudolfinum. It is so realistic that the artist may have taken a photograph to produce it. Printed by Minerva, thought to be printed in Czechoslovakia. Posted in Prague, possibly early 1900s.

Act II, Scene 2
The Cartoon

Like the British Naughty Seaside Postcard, the cartoon postcard was universally popular in all countries, particularly those with the street entertainment tradition.

Postcard 1

A modern card, date unknown. The legend on the obverse is Coastal Colour with a reference to Clacton on Sea.

Postcard 2

This is a Davis Brothers Pictorial postcard from originals by John Halls. It is one of a series entitled Popular Songs Illustrated, dated about 1904. The theme is, of course, 'The Lost Chord'

A Picture Postcard Play

Newspaper Headlines.
"FOREIGN AFFAIRS."

After the black & white drawing by John Hassall.

Dont turn the organ man. away. A. R.

Postcard 3

Again about 1904. A Raphael Tuck 'Oilette' series entitled 'Newspaper Headlines No.764, Foreign Affaires'. The term 'Oilette' seems to refer to the finish of the card because others made by them are marked Photochrome, Rapholette, Silverette, Gem Glosso, etc.

Postcard 4

A US postcard thought to be early 20th century. Note the organ grinder's peg leg and the monkey climbing up the legend 'A Musical Turn', an unsubtle attempt at humour!

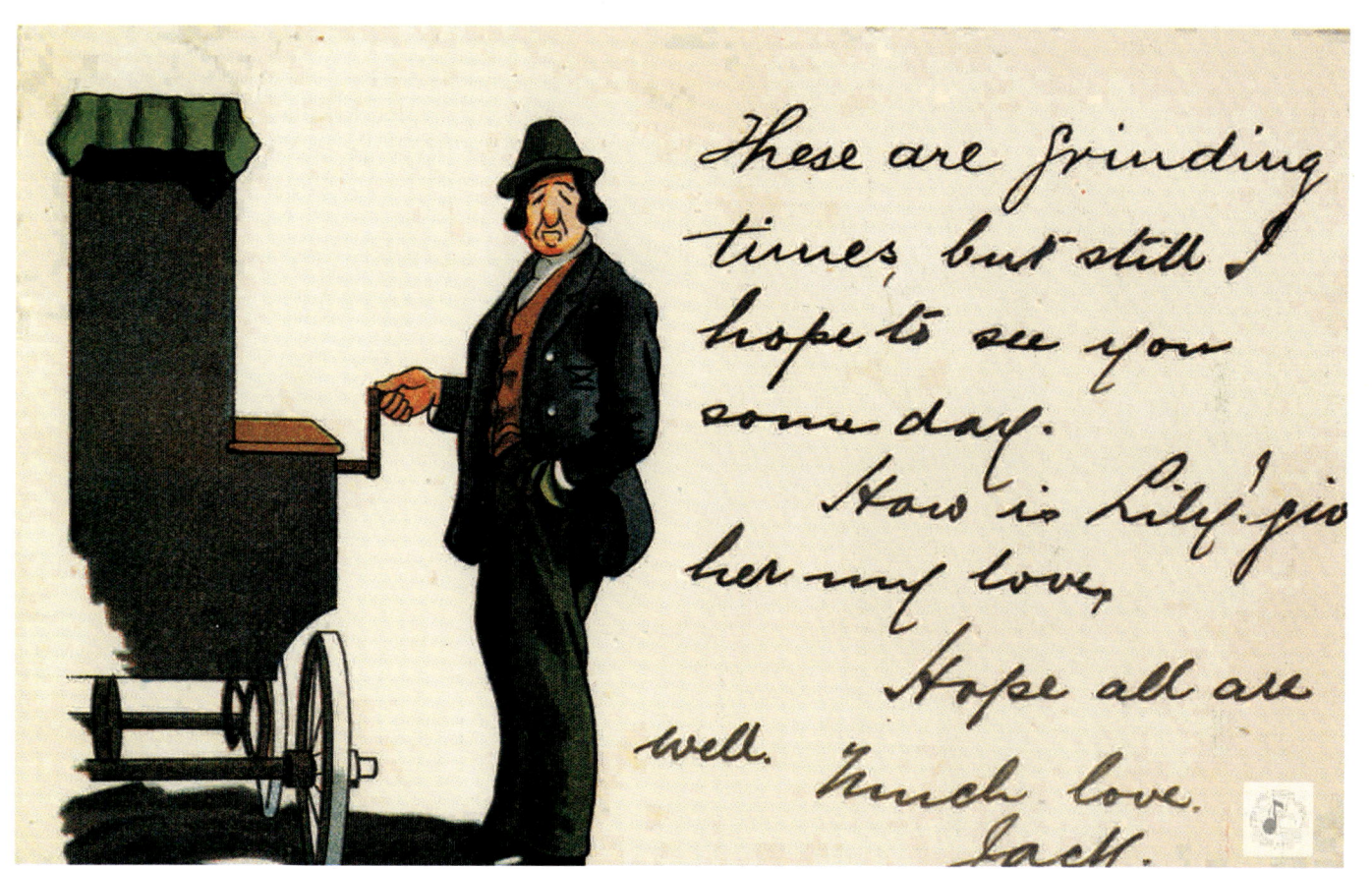

These are grinding times, but still I hope to see you some day. How is Lily? give her my love, Hope all are well. Much love. Jack.

Postcard 5

Circa 1904, series 80/3 of W. & A. K. Johnston of Edinburgh and London. Postcards were originally restricted to the obverse side being used for the address (on the right) and a small space for greetings on the left. The cartoon in this version allows for new regulations in the UK where the front can also be used for the message. This clever design appears to show the organ grinder as the author of the words written by Jack! The obverse states in print that this writing only applies to inland mail, not to foreign postage, according to Post Office Regulations.

Street Musicians on Postcards

A Picture Postcard Play

Postcard 6

An unusual postcard printed by a company with the monogram AH in a ribbon-twist cartouche. The obverse has the words Postcard written in several languages. Posted in Bedford city USA in 1907, the sender writes on the front 'I don't know what I playing but I playing some, Trace' (or is it Grace?). The address is a PO Box number.

Postcard 5

The writer says "Dear Brown Owl, we did enjoy the party on Saturday. We hope you got home without getting wet (sic) with love from Dorothy and the Brownies" Drawn by Margaret Tempest and (wrongly) entitled The Hurdy Gurdy. Printed by the Medici Society Ltd. London, Pkt No. 77/5132; also in the USA by Hale, Cushman & Flint Inc. of Boston. Posted in 1941

Act II, Scene 3
The Organ Grinder

This small selection of novelty postcards is part of a set of ten, seven of which depict vignettes of the street musician. It was made in Germany in about 1980 as a special order from earlier postcard originals. They were clearly intended for an international market because the obverse side of each card is written in six other languages.

Postcard 1

Signed Nacthstuck, this card has a small cartouche for the sender to write on the front as well as the back. There is a collage of six scenes, the lower left depicting the 'busker' pointing out the words of the song. It is typical of the European scene; the words are also a little risqué.

Postcard 2

Another song, a group of comic characters making their way to Seckbach.

Postcard 3

This fairground scene shows the same two characters as in fig 1. Small print says it is a lithograph by Bruno Burger, Leipzig.

Postcard 4

This drawing is by Ottmar Zieher, Munchen (Munich). Behind the circular cartouche is a scene depicting an organ grinder. Again, the words are typical double entendre.

Postcard 5

Another lithograph, by Bruno Burger & Ottillie, Leipzig, depicting a lively fairground scene.

Street Musicians on Postcards

A Picture Postcard Play

Postcard 6

This café scene has the caption 'An organ grinder' but in French. Thus it is described as an 'Orgue de Barbarie'.

Postcard 7

Another lithograph, this time by Jiwalt & Ewald. This scene depicts the organ grinder using the organ as a means of attracting an audience to a fairground sideshow. This is the way the organ was first used before it became part of the carousel ride. The rectangular cartouche is left blank for the sender to write a message.

Act II, Scene 4
The Foreign Comic Postcard

Humour spans all cultures. Some postcards were produced for the local market but many an entrepreneur, particularly Germany and Czechoslovakia, produced cards for the international market. Here is a small selection:

Postcard 1

Posted in 1903, this coloured card is one of a series entitled Bohmische Volksleider (Bohemian folk singers), No. 6

Postcard 2

Posted in Norway in 1913 but produced for an international market, this maker is unknown but the series is Kunsterleben (meaning art experience) No.925.

Postcard 3

Maker and country unknown, identified only by H&S and thought to be Dutch. Dated 1912.

Postcard 4

Posted in Berlin in 1904 and produced for the international market. It is thought to be German, with an inscription B. K. W. 1602 – 8.

Street Musicians on Postcards

Å kiste=kla=ang!

Elfsborgsvisan.

Jag hafver mörrrdat ett barn för dig,
Du kunde väl ha förlåtet mig —
Men tjäderleken ä' lika stor
Hos fången, som på Elfsborg bor.

Postcard 5

A Picture Postcard Play

The Maker and country unknown but made for the international market. This quality card is printed and the figures embossed to give a 3D effect. Early 1900s.

A Picture Postcard Play

Czechoslovakian. Early 1900s.

Postcard 6

Postcard 7

Three black & white Czechoslovakian cards. Early 1900s

Second Intermission
The Story of Christie's Old Organ.

In 1874, the story of an orphan boy called Christie and an old beggar called Treffy, who roamed the streets playing a barrel organ, was one of the most popular and widely read of those times. It is little wonder that picture postcards featured barrel organs and pianos, no doubt owing much to the story of Christies Old Organ, or Home Sweet Home as it was first called. Until recent times, the author, Mrs. O. F. Walton, remained largely unknown and yet she was a prolific writer in the Victorian religious story tradition. Not so popular now-a-days, this type of writing was greatly in vogue. Christies Old Organ was translated into many languages. The initials O. F. were that of her husband, a vicar. Her real name was Amy Catherine, né Deck.

Born on 6th July 1849, her father was the reverend Deck, an evangelical vicar of St. Stephen's church, Spring Hill Street, Hull. Her first book, 'My Mates and I', was published by the Religious tract Society (RTS) in 1870 under her father's name. The RTS paid £24, a lot of money in those days. Her earliest books were then published anonymously but were so popular that she was granted the honour of publishing under her married name, never her own! Such was the subordination of most women in those times. The following year she married Octavius Frank Walton. She was 25 and he 30. Octavius took his divinity degree at Cambridge, a centre of evangelism, and became curate of St. Stephens in 1873. Amy spent her early years in Kingston-upon-Hull, to give this Northern city its full name.

Society at large was undergoing change in the 1870s. Hull, like many towns, was expanding into and destroying the countryside. Migrants from country to town fell out of the habit of going to church. Family ties were broken. Bright city lights caused people to 'succumb to sin'. There was also extreme poverty and deprivation. Mrs. Walton wrote about these themes, endeavouring to re-convert back-sliders. Her stories, or tracts, were morality tales of religious sentimentality based upon a simple and naïve belief that the country reflected beauty, purity and goodness. The towns contained poverty, drunkenness, ugliness and sin. A mother neglects her child and the child accidentally burns to death! ("My Little Corner"). Powerful stuff for the impressionable.

1874 was coincident with Luke Fielde's exhibition of his painting "Applicants for admission to a casual ward" depicting a hapless child helping a poor old man, a similar scene to that described earlier by Charles Dickens (1812-70) in The Old Curiosity Shop. It is thought this may have inspired Amy's story of Christie. Another feature of the story, not pinned onto the barrel of his organ, is the hymn

Street Musicians on Postcards

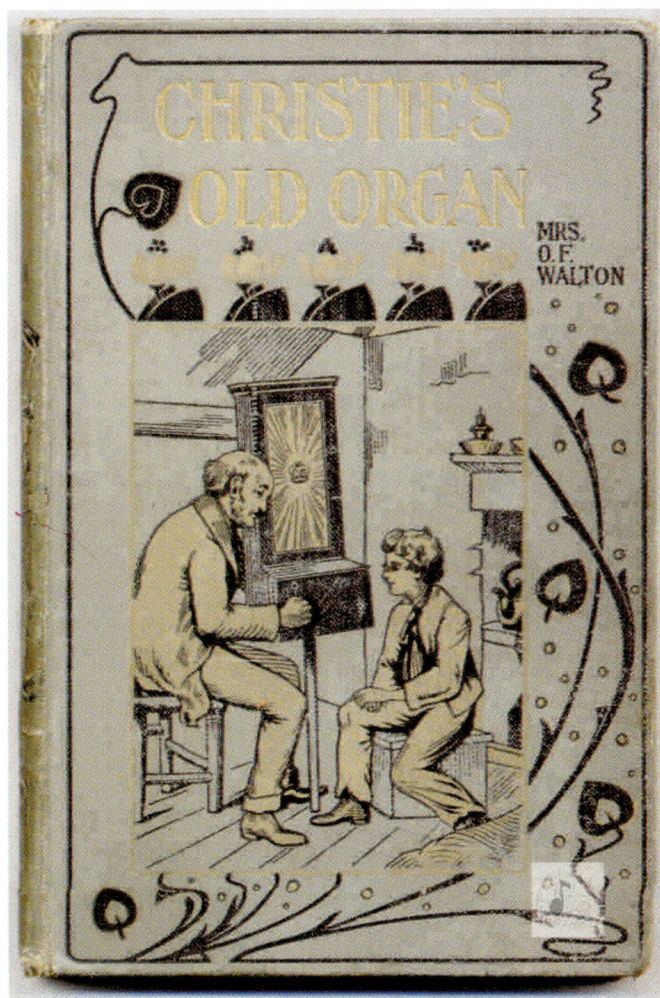

Fig.1

A Picture Postcard Play

"There is a City Bright". Each of its four verses is a theme for a chapter, a clever way to tell a story even if the story is really a sermon. This echoes the view of G. H. Spinney describing these tracts as 'Sheep in wolves clothing'. Thus, for the last verse, dying old Treffy, Christie's organ grinder master from whom he inherits the organ, is converted to the faith just before he expires! And, for good measure, Home Sweet Home is the last tune Christie's mother had sung before she departed to her eternal home! Fig.1 illustrates old Treffy in his attic, playing his instrument to young Christie.

Mrs. Walton and her husband began to travel widely soon after they married in 1875. Firstly, an appointment at mount Zion, Jerusalem until 1879, possibly as private chaplain to Murray Stewart esquire who heralded from Cally, Kirkcudbrightshire on the west coast of Scotland. They returned to Scotland to take up a 'living' in this locality, staying until 1883. Then another living for ten years at St. Thomas', York, next to an Industrial School for Girls in an area that had much scope for their evangelical zeal. Was our Amy sympathetic to her contemporary, Emmeline Pankhurst (1858-1928), the militant suffragette? In 1893, the Waltons move to Wolverhampton, leaving in 1906 to settle in the Garden of England at Leigh (pronounced Lie) in Kent.

A Picture Postcard Play

Fig.2

Amy Catherine Walton is buried in the churchyard of that village, near Tonbridge. The Tonbridge Free Press recorded her death on Friday, 5th July 1939, the eve of her 90th birthday, as the widow of the former vicar of Leigh. Mrs. Walton seems to have been a very observant person. Her writings give detailed observations of her times. Thus, in one scene she writes about Mabel, the daughter of the upper class, with whom Christie had become friendly, despite the rigid class barriers of those times. Mabel says: "Oh organ-boy, don't play to-day. Mamma is ill in bed, and it makes her head ache." Christie stopped at once; he was just in the midst of "Home Sweet Home". The organ gave a melancholy wail as he suddenly stopped.

A melancholy wail! The dying breath of an organ stopped in mid-play as the bellows pressure collapsed and the pipes wailed to a halt, so aptly described by one who must have heard this happen. John Payne heard his song played on the street organs. Surely, Amy must have heard this tune, and 'The Old Hundredth', and 'Rule Britannia', and 'Poor Mary Ann' (sung to the Welsh air All Through the Night), all pinned on Treffy's organ. Did she hear a poor young beggar boy play this tune, stopped by someone in mid-play? We shall never know but we might guess this aptly described observation of expiration was part of her inspiration for young Christie. Fig.2 shows Mabel turning the organ, the illustration coming from an abridged children's version of the story.

Street Musicians on Postcards

A KIND-HEARTED FARMER'S WIFE TOOK PITY
ON THE TREMBLING OLD MAN

Fig.3

A Picture Postcard Play

Amy gave us an image of the street organ grinder that, like those of Dickens, now forms part of our psyche. Fig.3 is another illustration from the abridged book, showing Christie in earlier times, dressed shabbily in 'toffs' clothing.

Home Sweet Home was written in May 1823 for the opera Clari, or The Maid of Milan, by the composer Sir Henry Bishop. The libretto was by John Howard Payne (1791-1852). He was an American who had never had a proper home. Payne sold the libretto for a paltry sum and thus made no money from royalties. He later wrote with bitterness that he often heard the tune played on a street organ when he was homeless and hungry on travels in Europe. The opera, based on Jean Françoise Marmontel's story Laurette, was performed on 8th May 1823 at London's Covent Garden Theatre. The song was used as a leitmotiv, or theme song, occurring in various forms throughout the opera. It became very popular and fitted well with Mrs. Walton's favourite theme, the sweetness of home, particularly the home in the country. She used it as a metaphor for the Heavenly Home. Did she know that Bishop was a noted reprobate, womaniser, spendthrift and home-wrecker? It seems not. Part of Clari has:

"Mid pleasures and palaces though we may roam,
Be it ever so humble there's no place like home.
A charm from the skies seems to hallow us there,
Which, seek through the world, is ne'er met with elsewhere.
Home, home, sweet, sweet home!
There's no place like home! There's no place like home!"

This contrasts somewhat with the humbler verse probably alluded to by Mrs. Walton:
"A charm from the skies seems to hallow us there,
O, give me my lovely thatched cottage again.
No more from that cottage again will I roam.
Be it ever so humble, there's no place like home!"

The story of old Treffy and Christie was still being reprinted in the 1990s. The popularity of the organ grinder was reflected in another collecting medium other than the Postcard. The following are two examples. Fig. 4 is an advertising cigarette card by maker Lambert & Butler. It is part of a series called "London Characters – The Organ Grinder". The obverse describes the illustration as follows: "The Organ Grinder and his monkey belong to a less sophisticated age than the present, with its bands of unemployed musicians and 'tinned' music in various forms. The organist of the 'eighties was usually a native of Switzerland and his instrument was a worn-out organ, under the weight of which he could sometimes scarcely stagger. The quality of the music mattered little, however, for public interest centred, as a rule, on the poor shivering monkey clad in red coat and cap, with wizened hand stretched out for coppers which invariably came his way".

Of course, the organists were not from Switzerland but from Italy.

Fig. 5 is another advertising card, this time by The English & Scottish Joint Co-operative Wholesale Society. These were in their packets of tea. Entitled 'Victorian Days", the caption on the obverse is incorrectly entitled "The Hurdy-Gurdy Man" and states: "The wandering barrel-organ musician has now almost disappeared. He was generally from Naples and its environs – a cheery individual and a popular figure eagerly looked for on his weekly round of our villages and hamlets. He was always sure of a cup of tea from the cottagers. And you are sure of a cup of good tea that gives no bad tannin effects if you drink E. & S. C.W.S. Digestive Tea Tips."

Street Musicians on Postcards

LAMBERT & BUTLER'S CIGARETTES

"London Characters"—
THE ORGAN GRINDER

Fig.4

A Picture Postcard Play

IN VICTORIA'S DAYS

E. & S. C.W.S. DIGESTIVE TEA TIPS

Fig.5

Act III, Scene 1
The Anniversary

Anniversary greeting cards were very popular and celebrated in all cultures. Some were shown in earlier Scenes and these are a further selection of different anniversaries.

Postcard 1

This staged photograph shows a ragged child as an organ grinder, complete with monkey. Closer inspection of the 'organ' reveals a stage prop, merely a box covered with a rug and a huge winding handle. Clearly, the poor but smiling urchin conveys a message of joy with an inevitable end result for all of us: Like milestones on the road of life, May birthdays one by one, Point out the way to happiness, Till all your Journey's done. Not exactly a thought one would wish to receive on a birthday! Maker unknown, early 1900s.

Postcard 2

An Easter card, printed by the International Art Publishing Co. of Berlin and New York and posted in 1910 in the USA. The charming central cartouche of Easter chicks playing a very realistic copy of an organ is surrounded by an embossed border of 'lace'.

Street Musicians on Postcards

A Picture Postcard Play

A Happy New Year!

 כ'בעגלייט דעם יאהר אייך מיט מיט געזאַנג
כ'בעגעגנען איהם דערמיט
אויף גליק און פרייד און לעבענ'לאַנג
האָב איך פאַר אייך אַ קוויט! - ⸺

לשנה טובה תכתבו

Postcard 3

This beautiful lithograph shows a rather smart organ grinder with a cage of love birds sitting atop. Written in German Yiddish it says: I greet the New Year with song and hope of happiness and long life. Printed by Wilamsburg Post Card Co. of New York. Early 1900s.

Street Musicians on Postcards

A Picture Postcard Play

Early 1900s. The artist is Josef Eberte, Vienna and printed by Deutscher Schule-Verien (German School of Art association). The text conveys that the wretched world can be saved by Christ's death on the Cross, thus a Christian greetings card.

Postcard 4

Street Musicians on Postcards

A Picture Postcard Play

Postcard 5

Another German postcard, date unknown (possibly early 1900s) with the greeting: Happy New Year. The comic minstrels sing an uncomplimentary song that diamonds and pearls will not adorn her face.

Postcard 6

A French New Year postcard. Date and maker unknown.

Easter Greetings

Postcard 7

A photo montage of children's faces on an Easter egg. Maker unknown but probably of German or Czechoslovakian origin and printed for a world market, Serie (sic) 336.

Act III, Scene 2
Postcard Pictures & Paintings

Not all postcards were for fun. Some were more serious souvenirs. If one visits the museums and picture galleries of today, nothing has changed. There are still plenty on sale. Here is another small collection from the past:

Street Musicians on Postcards

A Picture Postcard Play

QUIDO MÁNES:
Starý miàdenec. - Vieux garçon.
Alter Junggeselle. - Old bachelor.

Galerie Rudolphinum.

Postcard 1

From the Galerie Rudolphinum this picture, entitled Old Bachelor by Guido Manes, is by an unknown maker with the logos MK & VKVK, No. 1015. He plays a serinette (meaning little canary), the pre-cursor of the street organ. It was used mainly by women to teach caged birds to sing. Many of these old instruments are still called serinettes even though they developed from reproducing bird song to play tunes that a bird was unlikely to sing. Date of postcard unknown.

Street Musicians on Postcards

A Picture Postcard Play

Postcard 2

In contrast, a modern Spanish card drawn by Elsie. The shawl and dress is embroidered and the card produced by PAI (Postales Artesanas Internationalles).

Street Musicians on Postcards

A Picture Postcard Play

The Old Hospital, Mermaid St., Rye.

From a Water Colour Drawing by W. H. Borrow.

Postcard 3

The Old Hospital, Mermaid Street, Rye, from a water colour by W. H. Borrow. The card is The B & W Series – Hastings. Date unknown. This famous old building exists today. Note the barrel organ on the steep hill behind the lady.

A Picture Postcard Play

An Italian black & white postcard of a portrait at the Museo Marini. Date of production unknown but quite modern.

Postcard 4

Street Musicians on Postcards

A Picture Postcard Play

Postcard 5

A black & white photograph of an oleograph from the Italian Museo Marini. Date of production unknown but quite modern. An oleograph is a picture printed in oil colours.

Act III, Scene 3
Advertising & Oddments

Advertising was one of the earliest uses of the postcard and examples are found throughout the entire postcard history.

Postcard 1

A realistic drawing of an Italian 'grinding' a barrel piano, used as a gift-parcel tag with the words 'Seasons greetings'. Date unknown but modern.

Postcard 2

A comic sketch by Carl Anderson, called Henry. Henry offers the monkey a lighted cigarette which it takes with a pair of tongs. How wise! This is a Kensitas Brand cigarette card for J. Wix & Sons Ltd, Kensitas House, London. It is no. 29 in the second series of 50. The obverse also offers an album for the princely sum of 2d (two pence). It also assures the smoker that the product will not affect, irritate or hurt the throat and will actually protect against irritation and cough! Such is the power of advertising over the gullible and ill informed. Actual date unknown but thought to be the latter part of the 1900s.

Postcard 3

A delightful advertisement by J. & P. Coats, cotton thread manufacturers. The organists appear to be competing with each other. One with the German tune Wacht am Rhein and the other with a French air, Boulanger March. The back of the card is a calendar for 1890.

A Picture Postcard Play

May 7-13

5¢
POSTCARDS

BON
APETIT

NAPA
CAL

National
POSTCARD WEEK

Postcard 4

A modern American postcard advertising National Postcard Week, circa 1989. The obverse of the card is a specific advert by Carol Brockield: 'I buy and sell postcards, etc.'

Street Musicians on Postcards

A Picture Postcard Play

Postcard 5

An unusual coloured picture of a roll-playing piano. Entitled 'the Modern St. Cecelia, it depicts 'The piano any one can play'. Those who have tried know that considerable skill and musical knowledge is required. The card advertises the Farrand Company, Makers, Detroit, London. The obverse is over-stamped by an agent Geo. Lincoln Parker, Pianos, 100 Boylston St., Boston. The card was made by Chilton Company, Philadelphia, No. 3245, 1909. Why Cecelian? – because the piano is a Farrand Cecelian of London, as inscribed under the keyboard cover!

A Picture Postcard Play

Postcard 6

Entitled: 'Colleen's, Ballymaclinton. Mc.Clinton's Town. Erected by the makers of Mc.Clinton's soap, Franco-British Exhibition'. This unusual coloured photographic advertising card of a Chiappa & Sons barrel piano is in the Valentine Card series, posted in 1908.

Y.M.C.A Week.

Postcard 7

Advertising for a good cause. This black & white photograph is inscribed 'Y. M. C. A. Week'. Maker unknown and possibly early 1900s.

Postcard 8

The maker of this card is unknown, the obverse simply having the words Post Card written in seven different languages but possibly early 1900s. Although the characters look foreign, they are collecting for The Children's Home and Orphanage.

Street Musicians on Postcards

A Picture Postcard Play

Postcard 9

This black & white photograph is of a rather elegant group of people. The postcard appears to be produced by an unknown maker to be personalised by a photographer's client. The obverse is over-stamped: Vere Holloway, Photographer, 35 Maxilla gardens, Ladbroke Grove, Notting Hill, W, I, D. The last three letters are a mystery but it is a London photographer, early Edwardian by the style of dress and the lady's head-band.

Act III, Scene 4
Gramophone Post Cards

The musical box was superseded by the gramophone but it took much longer to displace the street musician and his piano or organ. However, the gramophone also featured on post cards from the early 1900s due to its ever increasing popularity. The disc record was even transcribed, in miniature 78 rpm form, onto post cards by Raphael Tuck & Sons. They patented a process so that a brown wax impression of a record could be over-stamped on a postcard and played on a conventional gramophone. The postcards were their Oilette Series, produced with and without the record. Pictorially, the cards were not a success as practically all the illustration is obliterated by the record. They were (and still are when not kept absolutely flat) prone to distortion.

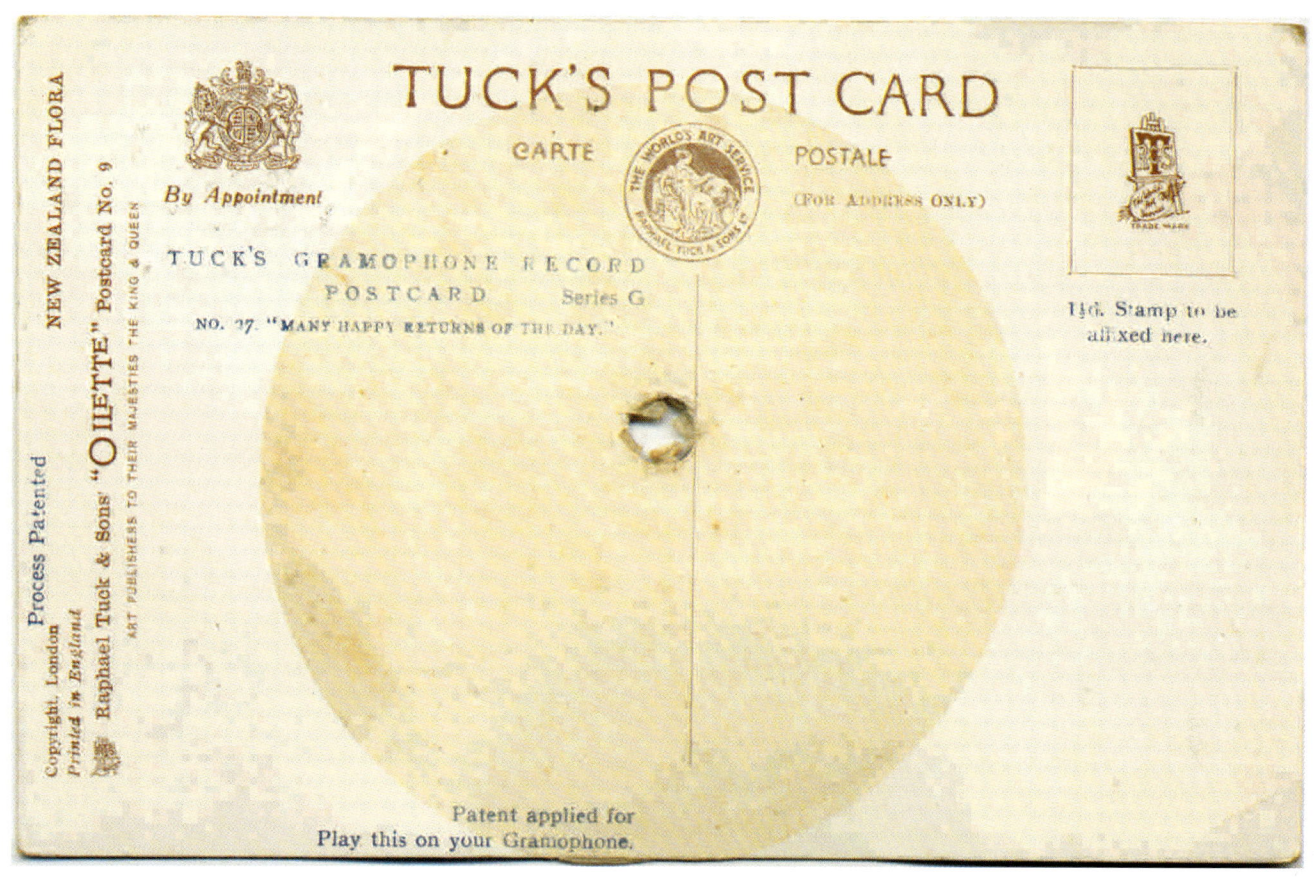

Postcard 1

This shows the obverse of each card which carries the standard Tuck inscriptions, including the Royal coat of arms and the words 'By Appointment'. Whilst the card also says 'patent applied for' it is then contradicted by the words 'process patented'. Either the format for the printing plates had already been prepared when applying for the patent, which then was approved just before production began, or the process constituted a different patent to the actual card. Another anomaly is that each record is inscribed with an alpha-numeric code that does not relate to either the series number or the tune number.

Postcard 2A

This shows the front view of a card to protect the actual post card. It states 'As an additional protection, place the enclosed protector with Tuck's gramophone record postcard in an envelope before addressing and posting.' This will explain why few cards are actually stamped or written upon. In fact, they are not meant to be used as a postcard in their own right.

Street Musicians on Postcards

Postcard 2B

A Picture Postcard Play

This shows the reverse side of the card with a list of tunes available for various occasions, seven series in all. Series B and G are birthday wishes, B with male voices and G with female voices. Series A, C and F are vocal, each with a selection of four tunes, all different. Series D has solo instruments, the cornet and saxophone. Series E is orchestral. Starting at series A, in alphabetical order, the tunes are uniquely numbered in sequence. Thus tune 1, 'Auld Lang Syne', is the first in series A and tune 12 'The Leather Bottel' (sic!) is the last in series E. Each series is sold in a pack of four cards at 1/- (one shilling) per pack. There were many other series in preparation following this particular issue.

Postcard 3

Oilette series No. 3586 is of racing greyhounds and has record No. 6.

Oilette series No 3253 is of strawberries and Series G No. 27, 'many happy returns'.

Postcard 4

A Picture Postcard Play

BRITANNIA STANDS FOR THE FREEDOM OF THE SEAS

Postcard 5

Oilette series P3262 is Britannia with the words 'Britannia stands for freedom of the seas'. This card is Series E No. 19. The obverse obviously had a particular emotional meaning because it carries the words: 'May the future make amends for the sacrifices of the past' and the verse by the playwright David Garrick: 'Still Britain shall triumph, her ships plough the sea, Her standard be justice, her watchword' be free', Then cheer up my lads, with one heart let us sing, Our soldiers, our sailors, our statesmen, our King'.

A Picture Postcard Play

In similar vein, a sailor bears the standard with the caption 'For the freedom of the seas'. This time, the obverse only has the first few line of Garrick verse, ending in "her watchword 'be free'".

Postcard 6

Street Musicians on Postcards

Postcard 7

A Picture Postcard Play

Oilette series No. 9 entitled 'New England Flora'. There is hardly any to be seen! The postcard is series G No. 27 again.

The End

A Picture Postcard Play

This beautiful etching is taken from Mother's Picture Alphabet, circa 1867, published in London by G. Watson of Kirby Street, Hatton Garden.

'O' BEGINS ORGAN

The Nicole Factor

(See Frontispiece for contact details)

The Nicole Factor tells the story of the Swiss musical box makers of the 19th century through the famous family of makers, Nicole. The story ends with the Nicole firm in London as the first British maker of gramophone records at the beginning of the 20th century. Included are two CDs, one with rare and fine recorded music played by an assortment of antique Nicole musical boxes and two early Nicole records, lasting 1 ¼ hours. The other CD is packed with pictures of old advertising catalogues. The Nicole Factor book has 250 art-quality pages with over 400 illustrations, 130 in colour.